Coratina

A Little Lost Olive On a Journey of Discovery

by

Orietta Gianjorio

Illustrated by Nathalie Fabri

Copyright© 2012 Orietta Gianjorio
All rights reserved.
ISBN-13: 978-1478227939
ISBN-10: 1478227931
First Edition: January 2013

CONTENTS

INTRODUCTION

Some time ago, I was sitting at my desk in front of my computer. I had been working for countless hours on a particularly challenging food and wine pairing book. I was exhausted.

All of a sudden, someone started talking to me. I wasn't sure if the voice I heard was my own or another's, but it was pushing for me to stop staring at the monitor, to look up and start using my imagination.

In my mind's eye, I saw a lovely and strong green olive. Her name was Coratina and she was alone in a foreign land. Without her family she had lost the ability to know who she was and discover her purpose in life. She had a smile on her face, dreamy eyes and long eyelashes.

Coratina came into my life to remind me that no matter how far we travel - physically or emotionally - how old we are or how successful we become, family - biological or adopted - is the only thing that gives us strength. Family, and the unconditional love they provide, is essential to making our stay on this earth worthwhile.

Therefore, this book is dedicated to families that still dine together, laugh together and read together. To my father who, throughout my childhood, read a new book to my brother and me every night. To my mother, who was unable to let her imagination run free because no one ever read a book to her. To my husband, a child at heart. And to the child we hope someday to have. To my beloved family in Italy and to the new one I found here. Two, ten or one hundred, family can be small or very big. The love they give is what matters.

Coratina is a lovely green olive.

She is stylish and *pretty*.

She wears a VERY elegant dress

and HIGH HEELS.

Coratina is small but **STRONG**

and very *adaptable*.

Coratina has *LONG* eyelashes.
She *flaps* her *LONG* eyelashes
every so often, **particularly** when she thinks.

Coratina lives alone in a small olive tree on the Mediterranean Coast.

She feels lonely because she can't find ANYBODY like *her*.

Coratina looks and looks. All day and NIGHt. Nothing. Nobody.

Coratina looks and looks. All NIGHt and day Nobody. Nothing.

One SUNNY day, **sitting** on the small olive tree, *Coratina* thinks and *flaps* her *LONG* eyelashes.

"It would be *nice* to have a FAMILY.

They could help me understand my *PURPOSE* in life."

Coratina thinks and thinks.

Coratina flaps and flaps.

Finally, *Coratina* **DECIDES**.

"I will travel the **WORLD** to find MY FAMILY!!!"

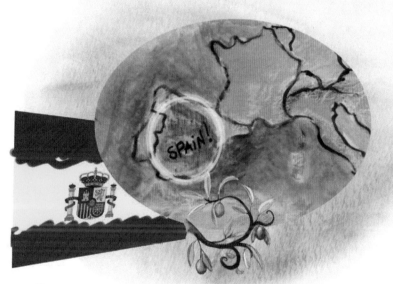

Coratina **DECIDES** to go to **SPAIN** first.

Coratina arrives in MADRID. In PLAZA MAYOR, she sees a *family* of olives. Mamá aceituna, PAPÁ ACEITUNA and dos pequeñas aceitunas. "Maybe they are MY FAMILY!" Coratina thinks, smiling and flapping her LONG eyelashes.

She moves closer and says: "Discúlpeme. Who are you? What is your name?"

Mamá aceituna answers: "Hola. Our name is ARBEQUINA. We are the MOST POPULAR olives in SPAIN! We are pequeñas but VERY RESILIENT. Everything we make is of high quality. Everything we make is AROMATIC and fruity. Everything we make has the fragrance of ripe apple, butter and ALMOND. Everything we make is quite mild."

Coratina looks at THEM, *flaps* her *LONG* eyelashes and thinks: "They **seem** nice, but I'm **NOT** like THEM! This is **NOT** my FAMILY! I better look elsewhere!"

She says: "GRACIAS Y ADIÓS," and she **WALKS** away...

Coratina **DECIDES** to go to *FRANCE*

in search of her FAMILY...

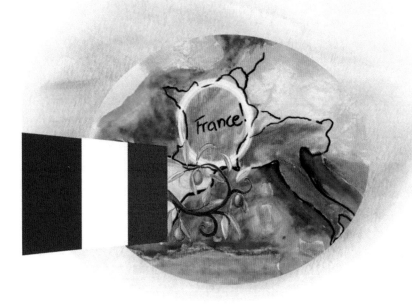

Coratina arrives in Paris. She sits at a café, looking at La Tour Eiffel. She flaps her LONG eyelashes and thinks: "This is an Elegant Country! I think I will **find** MY FAMILY today!"

While *Coratina* is still thinking, a beautiful little olive walks by. Coratina jumps on her chair, flaps her LONG eyelashes and thinks: "She could be MY SISTER!"

"*Pardonnez moi,*" *Coratina* says. "Who are you? What is your name?"

The beautiful little olive turns around and with a soft voice replies: "Je m'appelle Picholine. I'm the most popular olive in FRANCE! There are not many like me. I'm VERY STRONG but I'm also reserved. I don't like to travel abroad. Everything I make is delicate. Everything I make smells like ripe banana and ripe apple."

Coratina looks at her, flaps her *LONG* eyelashes and thinks: "I'm **NOT** like her. This *Elegant Country* is **NOT** my HOME. I better look elsewhere."

She says: "*Merci et au revoir,*" and she **WALKS** away...

Coratina is small but **STRONG,** *she* doesn't give up easily.

Coratina **DECIDES** to go to

GREECE in search of her FAMILY...

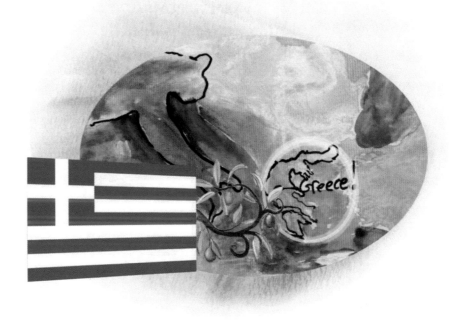

There, *Coratina* rests in the shade of the

PARTHENON.

From far, far away, *Coratina* sees an **old,**

HEAVY but small olive. "He could be

my *Pappou*!" she thinks and *flaps* her

LONG *eyelashes*.

"SIGNOMI!" *Coratina* loudly says. "Who are you? What is your name?"

The *old*, **HEAVY** but small olive slowly **MOVES CLOSER**.

The *old*, **HEAVY** but small olive slowly squats to sit in the shade near *Coratina.*

Looking at the PARTHENON, he says: "I have been **around** for a LONG **time**. My name is KORONEIKI. **EVERYBODY** knows *ME*. **EVERYTHING** I make is STABLE. **EVERYTHING** I make has a LONG **life**. **EVERYTHING** I make

has an *aromatic scent*.

EVERYTHING I make is not very pungent or **bitter**."

Coratina flaps her LONG eyelashes and thinks: "I would like to have a **Pappou!** But this is not MY **Pappou!** I better look elsewhere!"

She says: "EFHARISTO, YIA-SOU," and she

WALKS away...

Coratina flaps her LONG eyelashes and thinks: "I once heard of a COuntRy where EVERYTHING is possible. Maybe, There I will find MY FAMILY!"

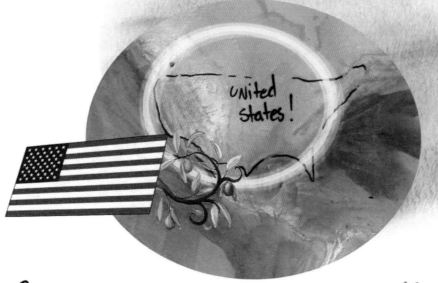

Coratina DECIDES to go to the United STateS in search of her FAMILY...

Coratina arrives in **California** and decides to REST ON THE BEACH. While she is *sleeping* under her UMBRELLA, *she feels* a SPLASH of water. She opens her eyes and sees a handsome olive on **a surfboard**.

"He sure is good looking!" Coratina thinks and flaps her LONG eyelashes.

"What'up?" Coratina says. "How's it going? And your name is...?"

The handsome olive puts the surfboard under his arm and JOGS over to Coratina.

"How's it shakin' baby?" The handsome olive says. "The Ladies call me Manzanillo. I'm a "California-style olive." I have to watch it on the board because I bruise easily.

I mature early, and everything I make smells cool.

Everything I make has a mellow personality.......

and mostly **I CHILL OUT!** Do **you** want **to CHILL WITH ME?**"

Coratina *flaps* her *LONG* eyelashes and thinks: "I don't know what **CHILL** means! He is definitely handsome but I can't **surf!** I better l**oo**k elsewhere!"

Coratina says: "take it easy! Hang loose! SEE YOU LATER ALLIGATOR!" and she **WALKS** away...

Coratina *is tired*.

Coratina *is sad*.

She flaps her LONG eyelashes and Wonders: "EVERYBODY I met makes SOMETHING! I don't know how to make anything!"

Coratina is sad.

Coratina is tired.

She flaps her LONG eyelashes and Wonders: "Will 1 EVER find MY FAMILY?"

Coratina **DECIDES** to l👀k at one LAST PLACE, and she goes **ALL THE WAY** to SUNNY ITALY in search of her FAMILY...

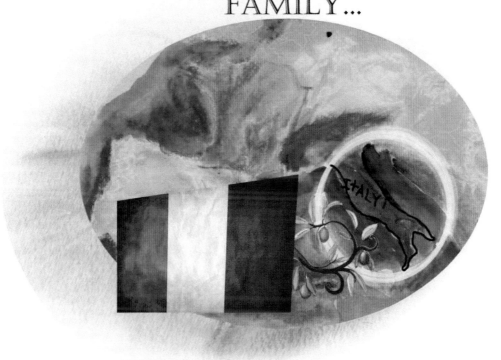

Coratina drives and drives.

All day and All **NIGHT**.
Nothing. Nobody.

Coratina searches and searches.

All **NIGHT** and All day.
Nobody. **Nothing**.

Coratina drives from *Fashionable Milan* to ANCIENT ROME...

From COLORFUL NAPLES to *Puglia*, at the end of the HEEL of the BOOT that is ITALY.

Coratina is **EXHAUSTED.**

Finally, *she* **stops** the car and sits under

a TREE on the side of the road.

Coratina flaps her LONG eyelashes and reads:
"Benvenuti a Corato"

Coratina flaps her LONG eyelashes.

She flaps her LONG eyelashes…

…flaps her LONG eyelashes…and

Coratina falls asleep.

Moments later, a stylish olive -

wearing an elegant suit and tie - walks by.

HE is small but **STRONG** and very *adaptable*.
HE has *LONG* eyelashes. HE flaps his *LONG*
eyelashes every so often, **particularly** when HE
thinks.

HE looks at *Coratina* and **STOPS SUDDENLY.**

Then HE turns around
and **calls:**

"*Cora!* Ho trovato *Coratina*!!"

A *lovely* and stylish
green olive
- wearing a very elegant dress
and HIGH HEELS -comes running.

She is small but **STRONG**
and very *adaptable*.

She has *LONG* eyelashes.

She flaps her *LONG* eyelashes

every so often, **particularly**
when *she* thinks.

The *lovely* and stylish green

olive looks at *Coratina*, *flaps* her

LONG *eyelashes* and *says* to her

HUSBAND:

"*Coro*, é *Coratina!!!*"

Coratina wakes up and looks at the two lovely and stylish green olives. She flaps her LONG eyelashes and says: "Mamma Cora, PAPÁ Coro! Is it you? I found you! I'm so Happy!"

Mamma Cora, PAPÁ Coro and Coratina are 3 lovely and stylish green olives. . . . .

and they **hug** for a

veeeeeeeeeery
loooooooooooooooooooooooooong
time.

Mamma Cora flaps her LONG eyelashes and softly says: "Coratina we were waiting for you! Today we are going to a VERY SPECIAL PARTY! Get ready. We are LEAVING in a few MINUTES."

Mamma Cora, PAPÁ Coro and Coratina walk to the PIAZZA CENTRALE. Under the Campanile, there are hundreds of lovely and stylish green olives

dancing and singing.

They are small but STRONG and very adaptable. They have LONG eyelashes. They all flap their LONG eyelashes every so often, particularly when they think.

Coratina meets NONNO SERGIO and Nonna Fiorenza.

Coratina meets **Zio Angelo** and Zia Agnese.

Coratina meets CUGINO GEPPETTO and Cugina Gessyca.

Coratina is so HAPPY! FINALLY, *she* is with HER FAMILY!

Mamma Cora flaps her LONG eyelashes and softly says: "Coratina, FOR CENTURIES, every year, at this VERY SPECIAL PARTY, our FAMILY comes together to make SOMETHING. A special gift - the gift of health and longevity for ALL PEOPLE everywhere."

Coratina JUMPS WITH JOY!

She flaps her *LONG* eyelashes and says:

"I WILL MAKE SOMETHING!
Just like **EVERYBODY ELSE** I met! I
WILL MAKE SOMETHING!"

Coratina is so HAPPY! FINALLY, she WILL MAKE SOMETHING! Coratina is so HAPPY! FINALLY, she knows her purpose in life!

Coratina flaps her *LONG* eyelashes and says:

"I want my gift to be **intense** and fruity. I want my gift to be pungent and bitter. I want my gift to have a LONG LIFE. I want my gift to have the *fragrance* of grass, cherry, APPLE and almond."

Mamma **Cora** and **PAPÁ** *Coro* look at each other and *flap* their *LONG* eyelashes. Their **Coratina** is now with HER FAMILY, *she* has her very own tree, and every year she can bask in the SUN

until ....

.........it's time to go to the VERY SPECIAL PARTY all over *again!* THERE, *Coratina* will **dance** and *sing* with HER FAMILY, and **make another special gift.**

Coratina is HAPPY.
Coratina JUMPS WITH JOY!

Coratina smiles, *flaps* her *LONG* eyelashes and *says:*

"ARRIVEDERCI!

See you next year!"

Olive Varietals

For all of you reading this book to your children, grandchildren, nieces and nephews or other little friends, I put together a small section to briefly explain olive oil and the different olive varietals, some of which are featured as characters in this book.

The *Olea europaea sativa* (olive tree) is a domesticated varietal of the wild *Oleaceae* family. This evergreen and long-lived tree was first domesticated in the Eastern Mediterranean between 8,000 and 6,000 years ago. The olive tree is very resilient and flexible to different soils and climate conditions. Its only vulnerability is freezing temperatures.

The olive tree has many different varieties (specifically called *cultivars*). Some cultivars are *autochthonous* (native) to a certain place and acquire a specific personality only in that *terroir*[1]. If cultivars are planted in any other area rather than their native place, they are prone to develop a different personality.

The fruit of the olive tree (olives) are harvested at different times, according to their intended use: making oil or curing. For olive oil, olives can be picked green, *in veraison* (when the skin turns red-purple in color), or black. The choice depends on the cultivar and the oil style. Generally, in the northern hemisphere, harvesting occurs from October to January (with the peak season in November and December). Olive oil is a liquid fat extracted by centrifuging the paste of crushed olives, and it has been produced for centuries, especially in the Mediterranean countries.

Olive oil personality is influenced by many aspects, including harvesting time and production techniques, but the most important aspect is the olive cultivar. Just like grape varietals, olive cultivars do not determine quality, they only influence aromas and flavors of olive oil.

Here is a short list of the different cultivars, starting with the characters featured in this book:

---

[1] *Terroir* is a French term that signifies geography, geology and climate of a certain place.

Coratina is the main cultivar of Corato (a small town in Puglia - Italy).

The oil extracted from Coratina tends to have a very long shelf-life due to its high polyphenol content. It has a medium aromatic profile[2], a consistent bitterness and an intense pungency[3]. Typical aromas: grass, apple, cherry and almond.

ARBEQUINA is a cultivar native to Catalonia (Spain).

The oil extracted from Arbequina is of high quality, but it doesn't tend to have a long shelf-life due to its low polyphenol content. It has a strong aromatic profile, a low bitterness and pungency. Typical aromas: ripe apple, butter and almond.

Picholine is the main cultivar of France.

The oil extracted from Picholine is of very high quality and tends to have a long shelf-life due to its high polyphenol content. It has a medium fruity profile and a delicate taste because of a low bitterness and pungency. Typical aromas: ripe banana and ripe apple.

KORONEIKI is a cultivar native to Greece.

The oil extracted from Koroneiki tends to have a very long shelf-life due to its high polyphenol content. It has a strong fruity profile, a medium bitterness and pungency. Typical aromas: grass, green apple, banana and floral notes.

Manzanillo is the main cultivar in California, but it is originally from Andalucía (Spain)[4].

The oil extracted from Manzanillo is of good quality and tends to have a fairly long shelf-life due to its high polyphenol content. It has a medium bitterness but an intense pungency. Typical aromas: grass and pepper.

---

[2] An oil is described as having an *aromatic profile* if it is capable of delivering a wide set of olfactory sensations.

[3] An olive oil is considered *bitter* when it has a bitter taste. To understand this taste, think about drinking black coffee and eating chocolate with no sugar. An olive oil is considered *pungent* when it activates thermo and chemo sensitive receptors. To understand this sensation, think about eating black pepper, ginger and horseradish. Generally, bitterness and pungency are considered good qualities for an olive oil.

[4] The *Manzanillo* varietal is more often used to produce table olives.

OTHER OLIVE VARIETALS. *Arbosana* (Spain): This cultivar produces an oil with herbaceous aromas, some pungency and bitterness. *Ascolana* (Marche - Italy): This cultivar produces an oil with aromas of apricot and tomato leaf. *Barnea* (Israel and Australia): This cultivar produces an oil with mild bitterness and pungency. *Bosana* (Sardinia - Italy): This cultivar produces an oil with herbaceous aromas, medium bitterness and pungency. *Frantoio* (Tuscany - Italy): This cultivar produces a strong oil with some pungency and aromas of artichoke and grass. *Hojiblanca* (Andalucía - Spain): This cultivar produces an oil with low pungency and bitterness, aromas of grass, mint and ripe fruit. *Leccino* (Tuscany - Italy): This cultivar produces an oil with low bitterness and pungency, aromas of nuts, cinnamon and green tea. *Maurino* (Tuscany - Italy): This cultivar produces a good oil for blending, with strong aromas and spicy notes. *Moraiolo* (Tuscany - Italy): This cultivar produces an oil with strong herbaceous aromas, medium bitterness and pungency. *Pendolino* (Tuscany - Italy): This cultivar produces an oil with herbaceous aromas, medium to strong bitterness and pungency. *Picual* (Andalucía - Spain): This cultivar produces an oil with medium bitterness, aromas of flowers and tomato leaf. *Sevillano* (Spain): This cultivar produces a mild but very fruity oil, with aromas of flowers and nuts. *Taggiasca* (Liguria - Italy): In Italy, this cultivar has been picked overripe for centuries, and it has traditionally produced a delicate oil with mild aromas, low bitterness and pungency. Today, some producers are harvesting the olives at an earlier stage, creating an oil with a completely different profile.

TERMINOLOGY

Coratina is **Strong:** The tree is resilient.

Very Adaptable: The tree gives good results in different terroir.

Somewhere on the Mediterranean Coast: The olive tree is considered by many to be native to this area.

MOST POPULAR: The cultivar is commonly planted in that area.

We are pequeñas: The olives produced by this tree are small.

VERY RESILIENT: The tree is robust but flexible to different soils and climate conditions.

Everything we make is of *high quality:* The olive oil produced with this cultivar is of high quality.

Everything we make is AROMATIC and fruity: The olive oil produced with this cultivar has a wide set of olfactory sensations, some of which are reminiscent of fruit.

Everything we make has the *fragrance* of ripe apple, butter and ALMOND: The olive oil has aromas reminiscent of ripe apple, butter and almond.

Everything we make is quite mild: The olive oil produced with this cultivar is not very bitter or pungent.

There are **not** many like me: The cultivar is not planted in many parts of the world.

I'm VERY STRONG but I'm also reserved. I don't like to travel abroad: This tree is resilient, but it doesn't perform as well if planted anywhere other than its native area.

Everything I make is delicate: The olive oil produced with this cultivar has a delicate taste, low bitterness and pungency.

Everything I make smells like ripe banana and RIPE APPLE: The olive oil has aromas reminiscent of ripe banana and ripe apple.

I have been around for a LONG time. EVERYBODY knows ME: This cultivar is old and very popular.

EVERYTHING I make is STABLE: The olive oil produced with this cultivar is stable in storage.

EVERYTHING I make has a LONG life: The olive oil produced with this cultivar has a long shelf-life, generally because it is high in polyphenols.

EVERYTHING I make has an *aromatic scent:* The olive oil produced with this cultivar has a strong aromatic profile.

EVERYTHING I make is not very pungent or **bitter:** The olive oil produced with this cultivar is slightly pungent and mildly bitter.

I **bruise easily:** Harvesting needs to be performed carefully because the olives can be easily damaged[5].

I **mature** early: The tree starts to bear fruit relatively early.

Everything I make SMELLS COOL: The olive oil produced with this cultivar has a wide set of olfactory sensations.

Everything I make has a *mellow personality:* The olive oil produced with this cultivar has low bitterness.

I mostly **CHILL OUT:** The tree is easy to plant and care for.

I want my **gift** to be **intense:** The aromas and flavors of the olive oil are very powerful.

And fruity: The aromas of the olive oil are reminiscent of fruit.

I want my **gift** to be **pungent** and **bitter:** The olive oil is pungent and bitter.

I want my **gift** to have a LONG LIFE: The olive oil has a long shelf-life.

---

[5] All cultivars have the tendency to bruise or break. If olives are damaged or if the olive oil is poorly handled, it could be the beginning of reactions capable of leading to a defective olive oil. For more information: *The Defects Wheel® For Olive Oil* (www.appliedsensory.com)

Have the *fragrance* of grass, cherry, apple, almond, banana and ARTICHOKE: The olive oil has aromas reminiscent of grass, cherry, apple, almond, banana and artichoke.

FOREIGN WORDS

PLAZA MAYOR: (Spain) The Main Square in Madrid.

Mamá: (Spanish) Mother.

PAPÁ: (Spanish) Father.

Aceituna: (Spanish) Olive.

Dos pequeñas aceitunas: (Spanish) Two Little Olives.

Discúlpeme: (Spanish) Excuse me.

Hola: (Spanish) Hi.

GRACIAS Y ADIÓS: (Spanish) Thanks and Goodbye.

Café: (French) Coffee House.

La Tour Eiffel: (France) The Eiffel Tower in Paris.

Pardonnez moi: (French) Excuse me.

Je m'appelle: (French) My name is.

Merci et au revoir: (French) Thanks and Goodbye.

Pappou: (Greek) Grandfather.

SIGNOMI: (Greek) Excuse me.

EFHARISTO. YIA-SOU: (Greek) Thanks and Goodbye.

What'up?: (Californian) How are you?

How's it going?: (Californian) How are you?

And your name is?: (Californian) What is your name?

How's it shakin' baby?: (Californian) How are you?

CHILL OUT!: (Californian) Relax.

take it easy!: (Californian) Try not to worry too much.

Hang loose: (Californian) Try not to do too much.

SEE YOU LATER ALLIGATOR: (Californian) See you soon.

Cora! Ho trovato *Coratina:* (Italian) Cora! I found Coratina.

Coro, é *Coratina:* (Italian) Coro, she is Coratina.

Mamma: (Italian) Mother.

PAPÁ: (Italian) Father.

PIAZZA CENTRALE: (Italian) Main Square.

Campanile: (Italian) The Bell Tower.

NONNO: (Italian) Grandfather.

Nonna: (Italian) Grandmother.

Zio: (Italian) Uncle.

Zia: (Italian) Aunt.

Cugino: (Italian) Male cousin.

Cugina: (Italian) Female cousin.

ORIETTA

Orietta Gianjorio was born and raised in Rome, Italy. She moved to California in 2008, to marry the love of her life, Jeff. She is passionate about helping Americans reconsider their approach to food. Her motto is "forget the *nonsense* and retrain the senses." The "nonsense" is today's beauty trends that promote counting calories, points or nutritional values, and the fast paced society that encourages consuming enormous portions of prepackaged food "on the go." She inspires others to consider food, wine and olive oil as an overall leisure activity to be experienced with the involvement of sight, smell and taste.

Orietta graduated *Summa Cum Laude* in Film Studies and has a Masters *Summa Cum Laude* in Cultural Journalism. She is a member of the *UC Davis Olive Oil Taste Panel*, she holds a diploma of *Sommelier*, and she is the Delegate in the greater Sacramento area for the *Accademia Italiana della Cucina* (*Italian Academy of Cuisine*). She wrote, produced and hosted several TV shows in Italy and America. Before moving to the US, she was the food & wine Editor for an Italian publication.

Today, Orietta is a regular guest on many TV stations and, besides leading sensory seminars, tastings, cooking classes and food & wine tours in Italy, she is working on her fourth book.

This is Orietta's first children's book and definitely not her last.

Nathalie

Nathalie Fabri was born to Belgian parents who traveled extensively around the world, and who collected many works of art. Her early memories of wanting to be an artist stemmed from observing the colors in these paintings.

Nathalie is a professional artist specializing in urban landscapes and loves to use her skills to work on children's book illustrations. She is the author and illustrator of *The Goats Were Everywhere* and has also created and published a children's magazine called *Broccoli Blue*.

When she is not creating art, Nathalie works as a French and Art teacher for kids and lives with her partner and young son in San Francisco.

THANK YOU

My dearest thanks and love, today and forever, to my family, my mom Fiorenza, my dad Sergio, my brother Angelo and, my husband, Jeffrey.

Thanks to illustrator Nathalie Fabri. She was able to transform this book into something really special. Thanks to Cheryl and Merritt (Marino) Moore for helping me find Nathalie.

A special thanks to Judith Faerron and Katie Gibbs. Thanks to Tania Fowler.

Thanks to the *Robert Mondavi Institute for Food and Wine Science* and particularly the *Olive Oil Taste Panel*, specifically the former leader Jean-Xavier Guinard, current leader Sue Langstaff, Dan Flynn, Nicole Sturzenberger, and all the other panel members. A special thanks to Amy Bridge Day.

Thanks to the *Associazione Italiana Sommelier*, and to the *Accademia Italiana della Cucina*, particularly the President Giovanni Ballarini, the General Secretary Paolo Petroni, and all the members of the Sacramento Delegation.

Thanks to *KCRA3*, particularly Michele Jeffrey, Mike Carroll and Richard Sharp; and to *FOX40*, particularly Natasha Lee.

Thanks to the *Italian Cultural Society* in Sacramento, particularly Patrizia and Bill Cerruti; the *Italian Cultural Center* in Los Angeles, particularly Ina Cohen and Massimo Sarti; the *Italy-America Chamber of Commerce* in Los Angeles, particularly Letizia Miccoli and Raffaele Rinaldi; and the *Sons of Italy*, particularly the Natomas Delegation.

A special thanks to my *Alfa Romeo Graduate*, Lola, for driving Coratina all around Italy.

RESOURCES

Dolamore, Anne. *The Essential Olive Oil Companion* (New York: Interlink Books, 1994).

Knickerbocker, Peggy. *Olive Oil from Tree to Table* (San Francisco: Chronicle Books, 1997).

www.appliedsensory.com

www.oliveoilsource.com

www.oliveoil.ucdavis.edu

www.agrolive.com

www.oliveoildigest.com

www.internationaloliveoil.org

www.oliveoiltimes.com

Hellenic Greek Center & Hall (Sacramento).

Made in the USA
San Bernardino, CA
24 August 2014